For Cheryll Black, the teacher who impacted me the most, early in my career and throughout - and simply the best teacher, ever.
— Frank

To my Mom who has always supported my dreams of being a teacher, and the one who first taught me to love others.
— Barbara

For Mom and Dad, my first and most important teachers
— Kayla

Acknowledgments

It takes so much effort from so many people to build a children's picture book—more than a village of creative and innovative minds. But for us, we'd like to acknowledge our incredible editor, Sarah Rockett. Sarah is a force! And Kayla Harren—her heart and her art illuminate our words and it is Kayla who creates the story in these "*like You*" books.
— Frank and Barbara

SLEEPING BEAR PRESS™

2395 South Huron Parkway, Suite 200, Ann Arbor, MI 48104
www.sleepingbearpress.com
© Sleeping Bear Press
Printed and bound in the United States.
10 9 8 7 6 5 4 3 2 1

Library of Congress Cataloging-in-Publication Data

Names: Murphy, Frank, 1966- author. | Dan, Barbara, author. | Harren, Kayla, illustrator.
Title: A teacher like you / by Frank Murphy and Barbara Dan ; illustrated by Kayla Harren.
Description: Ann Arbor, Michigan : Sleeping Bear Press, [2021] | Audience: Ages 6-10. | Summary: "Teachers can change the life of a child with every new day. Whether they're discovering math, practicing an instrument, or learning about our wonderful, diverse world, students can count on the kindness, innovation, and patience of a teacher. This is a celebration of the ways teachers help their students bloom"– Provided by publisher.
Identifiers: LCCN 2020039881 | ISBN 9781534111134 (hardcover)
Subjects: CYAC: Teachers–Fiction.
Classification: LCC PZ7.1.M8724 Te 2021 | DDC [E]–dc23
LC record available at https://lccn.loc.gov/2020039881

A TEACHER like YOU

By Frank Murphy and Barbara Dan

Illustrated by Kayla Harren

PUBLISHED BY SLEEPING BEAR PRESS

There are so many teachers in the world—

teachers of every

subject
and **style**.

But there's only one **teacher** like you.

And the world needs a teacher—just like you.

The world needs a teacher . . .
to be loving and accepting.
To be full of wonder and inspiration.

I needed a teacher like you.

Every day, you were happy to see us
and you always knew when I needed a hug.

You read us your favorites.
Together we soared through story after story.
Together we learned to see life from new perspectives.

You taught us to be creative
and to be proud of how we express ourselves.

The way we write our names.
The way we draw our dreams—and make them come true.
You encouraged us to make each day a masterpiece.

You practiced with us . . .

each problem or experiment.

Each swing or shot.

And each time I made a mistake,
you reminded me I was getting smarter.

Every step of the way, you reminded us
to set goals and make plans.
And that's how I succeeded.

When life got scary,
you were still there—

I needed a teacher like you.

With lessons that kept me focused.

Projects that let my imagination soar.

And reminders to breathe in and out . . . in and out.

You gave your time when you didn't have to.
Showing up at our games

and recitals.

You led us to volunteer.
Watching you give back
inspired us to give more.

Every day you created a safe place.
You let us be curious and taught us how to ask questions.

We felt confident to raise our hands.
You saw my potential.

I needed a teacher like you.

You shared your heart and made ours grow.
You listened . . . when no one else would.

You taught us to connect with each other.
You guided us to accept differences and value our own.

We learned to think before
we speak and act.
We learned we can't take
back what we say and do.

We learned to listen first.
We learned from watching you.

You taught us to be leaders.

You cared.
You comforted.

You challenged.
And you let me be me.

I needed a teacher like you.

You said I was smart . . .
so I was.

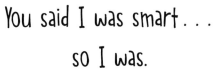

You said you believed in me . . .
so I did too.

You were a
hero to me.

And I hope you know,
the world needs teachers...

inspiring teachers,
accepting teachers,
loving teachers.

Teachers just like YOU!

Authors' Note

"I've learned that people will forget what you said, people will forget what you did, but people will never forget how you made them feel."— Maya Angelou

We can all recall that one teacher or mentor, the one we still talk about as adults, the one who left a lasting impression and shaped the way we think and act today. The world needs teachers like that. Children need teachers like that. And *A Teacher Like You* honors teachers of all kinds by highlighting the many ways teachers strive to make a difference in their students' lives.

A teacher's role in a child's life far exceeds academics. With every lesson there is always *another* lesson, or another piece of wisdom that we hope to impart. Teaching is layered with the wishes, desires, goals, hopes, and dreams we have for our students. Teachers act as counselors, nurses, confidants, and leaders for their students. Teachers are an integral part of our society. Teachers are essential!

Now, more than ever, we take time to honor the teachers, mentors, instructors, and coaches who have gone above and beyond. The ones who impart curriculum, but also help their students bloom and reach their full potential—whether on the field, in a classroom, or through a virtual platform.

We hope *A Teacher Like You* also gives voice to the many students who have come and gone through your classroom—the students who needed a hug to start their day, the kids who needed more practice, the children who needed that extra word of encouragement or kindness to get through a tough moment, the ones who needed someone to ask them what they wish for—this book was written for them as well. They needed a teacher like you.

– Frank Murphy and Barbara Dan